The
Three Little Wolves
and the
Big Bad Pig

EUGENE TRIVIZAS

ILLUSTRATED BY HELEN OXENBURY

EGMONT

For Grace
E.T.

In memory of
Stanley
H.O.

First published in Great Britain 1993
This edition published 2003
by Egmont Books Limited
239 Kensington High Street, London W8 6SA

1 3 5 7 9 10 8 6 4 2

Text copyright © Eugene Trivizas 1993
Illustrations copyright © Helen Oxenbury 1993
The author and illustrator have asserted their moral rights
A CIP catalogue record for this title is available from The British Library

ISBN 1 4052 0945 3

Printed in Italy

Once upon a time there were three cuddly little wolves with soft fur and fluffy tails who lived with their mother. The first was black, the second was grey and the third white.

One day the mother called the three little wolves round her and said, "My children, it is time for you to go out into the world. Go and build a house for yourselves. But beware of the big bad pig."

"Don't worry, Mother, we will watch out for him," said the three little wolves and they set off.

Soon they met a kangaroo who was pushing a
wheelbarrow full of red and yellow bricks.
"Please, will you give us some
of your bricks?" asked
the three little wolves.

"Certainly," said the kangaroo, and she gave them
lots of red and yellow bricks.
So the three little wolves built themselves a
house of bricks.

The very next day, the big bad pig came prowling
down the road and saw the house of bricks that
the little wolves had built.

The three little wolves were playing croquet
in the garden. When they saw
the big bad pig coming,
they ran inside the house
and locked the door.

The pig knocked on the door and grunted,
"Little wolves, little wolves, let me come in!"

"No, no, no," said the three little wolves. "By the
hair on our chinny-chin-chins, we will not let you
in, not for all the tea leaves in our china teapot!"

"Then I'll huff and I'll puff and I'll blow your house down!" said the pig.

So he huffed and he puffed and he puffed and he huffed, but the house didn't fall down.

But the pig wasn't called big and bad for nothing.
He went and fetched his sledgehammer and he
knocked the house down.

The three little wolves only
just managed to escape before the bricks
crumbled, and they were very frightened indeed.

"We shall have to build a stronger house," they said.
Just then, they saw a beaver who was mixing
concrete in a concrete mixer.

"Please, will you give us some of your concrete?"
asked the three little wolves.

"Certainly," said the beaver
and he gave them buckets
and buckets full of messy,
slurry concrete.

So the three wolves
built themselves a
house of concrete.

No sooner had they finished than the big bad pig came prowling down the road and saw the house of concrete that the little wolves had built.

They were playing battledore and shuttlecock in the garden and when they saw the big bad pig coming, they ran inside their house and shut the door.

The pig rang the bell and said, "Little frightened wolves, let me come in!"

"No, no, no," said the three little wolves. "By the hair on our chinny-chin-chins, we will not let you in, not for all the tea leaves in our china teapot."

"Then I'll huff and I'll puff and I'll blow your house down!" said the pig.

So he huffed and he puffed and he puffed and he huffed, but the house didn't fall down.

But the pig wasn't called big and bad for nothing.
He went and fetched his pneumatic drill and
smashed the house down.

The three little wolves managed to escape but their chinny-chin-chins were trembling and trembling and trembling.

"We shall build an even stronger house," they said, because they were very determined. Just then, they saw a lorry coming along the road carrying barbed wire, iron bars, armour plates and heavy metal padlocks.

"Please, will you give us some of your barbed wire, a few iron bars and armour plates, and some heavy metal padlocks?" they said to the rhinoceros who was driving the lorry.

"Sure," said the rhinoceros and gave them plenty of barbed wire, iron bars, armour plates and heavy metal padlocks. He also gave them some plexiglass and some reinforced steel chains because he was a generous and kind-hearted rhinoceros.

So the three little wolves built themselves an extremely strong house. It was the strongest, securest house one could possibly imagine. They felt very relaxed and absolutely safe.

The next day, the big bad pig came prowling along
the road as usual. The little wolves were playing
hopscotch in the garden. When they saw the big bad
pig coming, they ran inside their house, bolted the
door and locked all the sixty-seven padlocks.

The pig pressed the video entrance phone and
said, "Frightened little wolves with the trembling
chins, let me come in!"

"No, no, no!" said the little wolves.
"By the hair on our chinny-chin-
chins, we will not let you in, not
for all the tea leaves in our
china teapot."

"Then I'll huff and I'll puff and
I'll blow your house down!"
said the pig.

So he huffed and he
puffed and he puffed
and he huffed, but
the house didn't
fall down.

But the pig wasn't
called big and bad for
nothing. He brought
some dynamite, laid it
against the house,
lit the fuse and . . .

the house
blew up.

The little wolves
just managed to escape
with their fluffy tails scorched.

"Something must be wrong with our building materials," they said. "We have to try something different. But *what?*"

At that moment, they saw a flamingo bird coming along pushing a wheelbarrow full of flowers.

"Please, will you give us some flowers?" asked the little wolves.

"With pleasure," said the flamingo bird and gave them lots of flowers. So the three little wolves built themselves a house of flowers.

One wall was of marigolds, one wall of daffodils, one wall of pink roses and one wall of cherry blossom. The ceiling was made of sunflowers and the floor was a carpet of daisies. They had water lilies in their bathtub and buttercups in their fridge. It was a rather fragile house and it swayed in the wind, but it was very beautiful.

Next day, the big bad pig came prowling down the road and saw the house of flowers that the little wolves had built.

He rang the bluebell and said, "Little frightened wolves with the trembling chins and the scorched tails, let me come in!"

"No, no, no," said the three little wolves. "By the hair on our chinny-chin-chins, we will not let you in, not for all the tea leaves in our china teapot!"

"Then I'll huff and I'll puff and I'll blow your house down!" said the pig.

But as he took a deep breath, ready to huff and puff,
he smelled the soft scent of the flowers. It was
fantastic. And because the scent took his breath
away, the pig took another breath and then another.
Instead of huffing and puffing, he began to sniff.

He sniffed deeper and deeper until he was quite
filled with the fragrant scent. His heart became
tender and he realized how horrible he had been in
the past. In other words, he became a big *good* pig.
He started to sing and to dance the tarantella.

At first, the three little wolves were a bit worried, thinking that it might be a trick, but soon they realized that the pig had truly changed, so they came running out of the house. They introduced themselves and started playing games with him.

First they played pig-pog and then piggy-in-the-middle
and when they were all tired, they
invited him into the house.

They offered him china tea and strawberries
and wolfberries, and asked him to stay with
them as long as he wanted.
The pig accepted, and they all lived happily
together ever after.